ALF® THIS PLACE IS A ZOO!

Written by Robert Loren Fleming
Edited by Martha Kemplin

Designed by Pat Paris
Illustrated by Emily Kong, Karin Williams

CHECKERBOARD PRESS  NEW YORK

ISBN 002-689221-9

One sunny day, ALF found himself all alone in the backyard of the Tanner house. The rest of the family had gone on a picnic with friends. It was up to ALF to amuse himself at home for the day. The Tanners had only been gone a little while, but already ALF was bored.

He had already done all the fun things like...
looking for four-leaf clovers...

picking up big rocks
to see the ants and worms underneath...

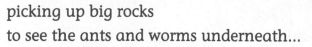

and hanging
upside down from a tree limb
until all the blood
rushed to his head.

ALF had even counted all of the pickets in the picket fence...three times!
"I've never been so bored in my entire life!" he thought to himself. "I wish
something exciting would happen to make the time go faster. *Anything!*"

Suddenly, ALF heard a strange noise coming from the bushes. When he crawled through the branches to investigate, he could hardly believe his eyes. There, coming through a hole in the fence, was an anteater!

Before ALF could stand up to move out of its way, the frightened anteater
leaped over the bushes. It scampered across the lawn toward the Tanner house.

Just as the anteater vanished into a cellar window of the house, two men jumped over the fence and dropped a big net over ALF's head! They were zoo janitors who had accidentally released Otto the Anteater from his cage at the zoo. The men were out searching the neighborhood for Otto when they saw ALF. After all, ALF did look a *little* like Otto–especially when he was on all fours!

"Hey! Yo! Wait!" ALF started to yell. But then he remembered that anteaters can't talk. If he said anything, the men might suspect the truth...that they'd accidentally captured an alien from space!

ALF bit his tongue and allowed himself to be carted off to the zoo. "This is just great," thought ALF to himself as he bumped along in the back of the zoo van. "Excitement I wanted, but this game of 'catch-the-furball' they can keep!"

At the zoo, ALF was tossed into the anteater cage. "Back home ya' go, Otto," said one of the men as the big door on the cage slammed shut.

"Yeah, and home, sweet home it *isn't*," muttered ALF to himself. "I gotta' get out of here – fast– it's almost lunchtime!"

The janitors were so relieved to have Otto back in his cage that they fed him his favorite meal...live ants! ALF had to eat some of the bugs so the men wouldn't get suspicious.

He spit the ants out as soon as the janitors left. "Pitooey! What miserable little morsels!" mumbled ALF under his breath. "But, a nice, juicy cat would taste good right now."

ALF's stomach was just starting to make hungry noises when he looked up and noticed Esmerelda, the female anteater who shared Otto's cage. She took one look at the furry alien and forgot all about her sweetheart, Otto. It was love at first sight!

Chased around and around the cage by the lovesick Esmerelda, ALF soon lost his appetite. "Back, back you hairy hussy!" ALF hissed at her. "I-I-I'm already taken. I've got three wives, forty kids, and I never pick the cat fur from between my teeth after meals," he lied. But Esmerelda continued to make eyes at him. Suddenly he understood why Otto had escaped!

Meanwhile, the Tanners arrived home to find ALF missing. But while searching for ALF in the basement, Brian discovered Otto. "Hey, this guy looks almost like ALF. Are you ALF's cousin?" he asked Otto as he peered at the animal in the dim light of the basement. Something about this creature was very different from ALF, but Brian wasn't quite sure what it was. When Otto moved into brighter light, Brian could then see what the difference was. This wasn't one of ALF's relatives – this little fellow was an anteater!

Brian coaxed the cold, hungry anteater upstairs with a box of chocolate-covered raisins. Otto ate them, but they weren't as good as the plain bugs he was fed at the zoo. In fact, the more Otto thought about it, nothing about this place was as good as the zoo. He even missed Esmerelda...a little bit.

Later, the Tanner's neighbor, Trevor, came over to ask why the truck from the zoo had been parked in front of their house earlier that day. The family quickly put two and two together. They figured out what must have happened to ALF.

The Tanners piled into the family station wagon with Otto and headed for the zoo.

By the time the Tanners arrived at the zoo, it was almost closing time. They found ALF in the anteater cage which was surrounded by a group of not-so-nice zoo visitors who were laughing at him and pelting him with peanuts.

"Spend one day in here being chased by a furry, flat-footed floozy and see what *you* look like!" said ALF under his breath to a man who had been jeering at him and pointing at his rumpled appearance.

Just then, ALF looked away to the other side of the crowd. And who did he see trying to push their way to the front but the Tanners! ALF was so happy to see his family that he gave Esmerelda a big hug!

Willie slipped around to the back of the cage. In the meantime, Kate, Lynn, and Brian distracted the zoo attendants.

Willie opened the cage door to set ALF free and return Otto to his rightful place. As ALF climbed into the empty backpack, he looked back to wave goodbye to Esmerelda, but the fickle anteater ignored him. She was already busy making eyes at her beloved Otto, who was making up for lost time by eating every ant in sight.

"Goodbye you two-timing tart!" yelled ALF. "And watch out, Otto, she's been on the track all day! Ha! Poor sucker, I hope he's in the mood for a good run!"

With that, Esmerelda started to chase Otto madly around the cage.

"Well, ALF," said Willie as he started the car, "looks like you had an exciting day after all."

"Yeah, right, but it taught me one thing," ALF replied. "I'll take home and boring any day. This place is a *zoo!* Ha!"